"Are you ready for your doctor's appointment, Blue?" asked Joe.
Today was the day for Blue's checkup with Dr. Maya.
"I guess so," said Blue. But she didn't sound too sure.

Blue was feeling a tiny bit nervous about her checkup.
"I wonder what will happen during my visit," she said quietly.
"What will Dr. Maya do?"

Blue's Checkup

Mrs. Leming

NICK JR

Blue's Clues

by Sarah Albee   illustrated by Ian Chernichaw

based on the teleplay by Jessica Lissy

SCHOLASTIC INC.

New York   Toronto   London   Auckland   Sydney

Mexico City   New Delhi   Hong Kong   Buenos Aires

Note to Parents from Creators:
It's time for Blue's checkup, but she's feeling a little bit nervous about visiting Dr. Maya. In this book your child goes to the doctor's office with Blue and Joe, and finds out that having a checkup isn't such a bad thing after all!

Based on the TV series *Blue's Clues*® created by Traci Paige Johnson, Todd Kessler, and Angela C. Santomero as seen on Nick Jr.®
On *Blue's Clues*, Joe is played by Donovan Patton. Photos by Joan Marcus.

ISBN 0-439-53915-3

12 11 10 9 8 7 6 5 4 3 2 1   3 4 5 6 7 8/0

Printed in the U.S.A.

First Scholastic printing, September 2003

"Let's pack some things to play with in the waiting room," Joe suggested.

"I'll bring Polka Dots and my doctor's bag," Blue said. "And Boris can come along too."

When they got to Dr. Maya's office, Joe said, "Well, here's the waiting room. So, let's wait!"

"We can play doctor while we're waiting," said Blue, taking out her doctor bag.

"Okay," said Joe, grinning. "Doctor! Doctor! My duck has an earache!"

Blue looked into Boris's ear with a special instrument. "I'll have him feeling better in a jiffy," she said as she bandaged Boris's ear.

"Thanks, Dr. Blue," said Joe.

Then it was Joe's turn to be the patient. "Doctor!" he cried. "I feel sick."

"Hmmm," said Dr. Blue. "I think you have a temperature. Take a nap, and call me tomorrow."

Just then they heard Nurse Kenny calling Blue's name.
It was her turn to go into the examining room.

First, Nurse Kenny checked to see how tall Blue had grown. Then h
weighed her. "You are growing very nicely, Blue," said Nurse Kenny.
"You are two feet tall. And you weigh twenty pounds."

Next Nurse Kenny checked Blue's blood pressure. He wrapped a cuff around Blue's arm and pumped air into it. Then he listened carefully to Blue's heartbeat.

"Does that hurt, Blue?" asked Joe.

Blue shook her head and giggled. "It feels like the cuff is hugging my arm."

Dr. Maya came in. "Hello, Blue! Hello, Joe!" she said. She washed and dried her hands at the sink, and then she put on her stethoscope. Dr. Maya asked Blue to take deep breaths as she listened carefully to Blue's chest and back. "Your heart and lungs sound terrific! Would you like to listen too, Joe?" asked Dr. Maya.

Joe put on the stethoscope. "Wow! I hear your heart!" he said excitedly. "It sounds like this, Blue: *Lub-dub, lub-dub!*"

"This is an otoscope," Dr. Maya explained. "Would you like to turn on the light?"

Blue pressed the switch, and a little light went on.

"It's dark inside your body. This light helps me see what's going on in there," said Dr. Maya as she peeked into Blue's ears, eyes, and mouth.

Next Dr. Maya asked Blue to lie back on the table. She pressed Blue's tummy all over, very gently. Then she helped Blue sit up again.

"You are such a good patient!" Dr. Maya exclaimed. "We are almost done with your checkup. The last thing we need to do is give you a shot.

"A shot?" Blue asked nervously.

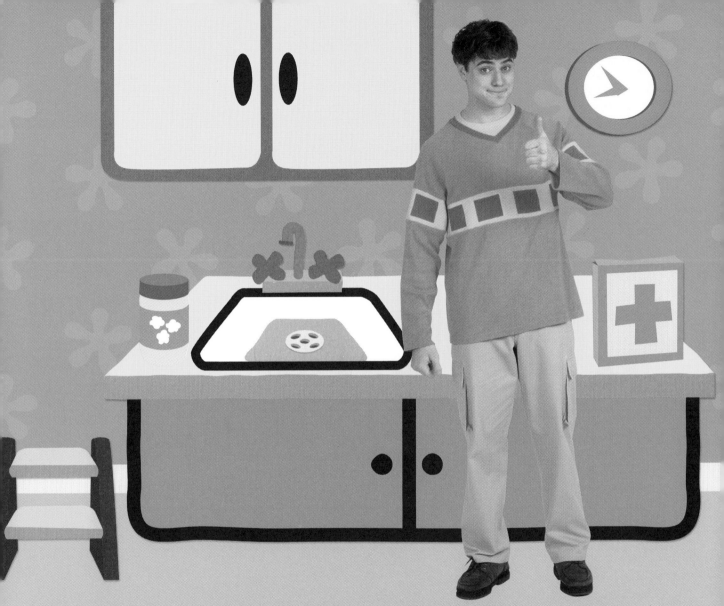

"Yes, Blue. The medicine inside the shot will help to keep you from getting sick," explained Dr. Maya. "You will only feel a tiny pinch. We'll count together like this: one, two, three, pinch—then it's over."

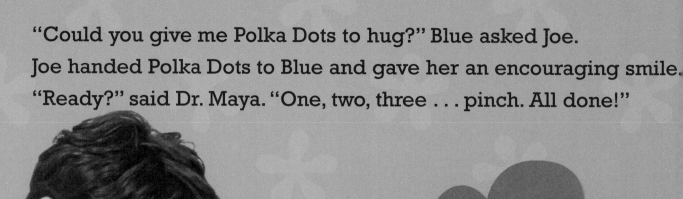

"Could you give me Polka Dots to hug?" Blue asked Joe.
Joe handed Polka Dots to Blue and gave her an encouraging smile.
"Ready?" said Dr. Maya. "One, two, three . . . pinch. All done!"

"Hey, that wasn't so bad!" said Blue.

Joe started to pack up their backpack while Dr. Maya reviewed another folder.

"Wait, don't go quite yet," Dr. Maya said as she read it over. "Hmmm Joe, it seems that *you* are due for a booster shot today."

"Me? A shot?!" asked Joe, surprised.

Nurse Kenny led him over to the examining table and cleaned his arm with a cotton ball.

"Here's Boris to hug," said Blue.

"Well," said Joe, "if Blue can be brave, then so can I." He clutched Boris tightly.

"Ready?" asked Dr. Maya. "One, two, three . . . pinch. All done!"

"You're right, Blue," said Joe. "That really wasn't so bad!"

"Good job!" said Dr. Maya. "Be sure to get a sticker at the front desk on your way out."

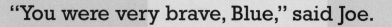

"You were very brave, Blue," said Joe.

"Thanks," said Blue. "So were you!"

"Thanks. Doctor Maya's a pretty cool doctor." Joe grinned.

"Come on. Let's go show everybody our stickers!"